*Esker Mike & His Wife, Agiluk*
*Scenes from Life in the Mackenzie River Delta*

# Esker Mike & His Wife, Agiluk

a play by Herschel Hardin

*Talonbooks . Vancouver . Los Angeles . 1973*

published with assistance from the Canada Council
and the Government of British Columbia through the
British Columbia Cultural Fund and the Western Canada
Lottery Foundation

*Talonbooks*                         *Talonbooks*
*201 1019 East Cordova*              *P.O. Box 42720*
*Vancouver*                          *Los Angeles*
*British Columbia V6A 1M8*           *California 90042*
*Canada*                             *U.S.A.*

This book was typeset by Donna Juliani, designed by
David Robinson and printed by Webcom for Talonbooks.

Fourth printing: April 1980

Talonplays are edited by Peter Hay.

*Esker Mike & His Wife, Agiluk* was first published in
*The Drama Review*.

Canadian Cataloguing in Publication Data

Hardin, Herschel, 1936—
    Esker Mike & his wife, Agiluk

    First published 1973.
    ISBN 0-88922-018-2 pa.

    I. Title.
PS8565.A72E8 1980       C812'.54       C80-091177-6
PR9199.3.H37E8 1980

33,405

# Introduction

The feminist magazine, *Ms.*, runs a regular column entitled "Lost Women." It is devoted to great women in history who could not realize their potential or were not given recognition, simply because they were not men. If Canada had a cultural magazine with a similar sense of mission, it might include a column called "Lost Playwrights." It would be about Canadians, of either sex, who could not and still cannot be produced on the Canadian stage, simply because they were or are not British, American, French, or anything — except what they are, Canadian.

One of the earliest columns would have to be devoted to Herschel Hardin, a lost playwright *par excellence.* After a dozen or so years of waiting for the Canadian Theatre to wake up to him, it is doubtful whether or not its wakening will come in time to persuade him to resume writing for the stage.

Since *Esker Mike & His Wife, Agiluk* was written during Canada's Centennial year, not one of the major theatres, subsidized annually to the tune of millions, has shown the slightest inclination to produce it. As I write this, none of them are planning to stage it, though artistic directors from coast to coast constantly decry the lack of "suitable" Canadian plays.

*Esker Mike & His Wife, Agiluk* was first published in New York in *The Drama Review*, one of the most prestigious theatre publications in the English language. That was in 1969. Hardin simply sent it in and the next thing he knew, it was printed. At that time, I was working for the Playhouse Theatre Company in Vancouver and even then I had a difficult time persuading the artistic director to read the script. One would have expected with a great American imprimatur, there would have been an orgy of productions in Canada, but there was nothing of the sort. It was not until the emergence of the Factory Lab Theatre in Toronto and the indigenous theatre movement that has burgeoned in the rest of Canada since, that the play finally has received some attention. The Factory Lab has, in fact, produced *Esker Mike* twice, and it has been staged here in Vancouver in a disused church by Troupe, as part of a Local Initiatives Project.

If *Esker Mike* were the only play that Herschel Hardin had written, there would be less grounds for pessimism. A four or five year lag between the creation and production of a play is not unusual even in countries where indigenous theatre is nurtured. The depressing fact is that a second completed work by Hardin, *The Great Wave of Civilization*, was written back in 1962 and still it has never been staged. A historical depiction of How the West Was Won, it was written with an ironic perspective unique to Canadian literature. That play won a Centennial prize in Alberta, before it was relegated to an already over-crowded oblivion. By the time Hardin finished working on the first part of another vast historical canvas, *William Lyon MacKenzie*, there was a brief lull in centennials, so there was not even a prize to be won. It is doubtful whether or not Part II of this third play will ever be completed.

6

The main reason that Hardin may not complete his third play is that he, like Shaw, turned to playwrighting for a similar reason: not to offer escapist entertainment for the middle classes who largely make up the audiences the world over, but to educate *and* even change them. Hardin wanted to use the stage as an enlarged soapbox on which he could expound certain ideas that he held. He saw the theatre as a public forum where he might share and discuss certain issues that were vital to him and his countrymen. When he found himself excluded from that forum, he accepted with resignation the fact that his plays were probably not good enough to be staged alongside the works of Shaw, or Brecht, or Arden, let alone instead of them, and he returned to journalism and broadcasting, branches of the media that have more informative power than the theatre as it now stands in this country.

What is really sad is that I suspect Hardin was right in considering the theatre the best platform for ideas that could change society, and that he was wrong in accepting the indifference he met from the so-called experts as a reflection on his work. His plays may not be as good as those of Shaw, but his work so far has been done at an age when the Irishman was writing only bad novels. Hardin, just like Arden, learned a great deal from the dramaturgy of Bertolt Brecht, but the characterization, humanity and ultimate durability of *Esker Mike* already go beyond most of the plays of the German dramatist. If the "experts" had given their attention and talent to Hardin in the way that he has given his to them, his name might be as familiar today to the Canadian theatre-going public as that of another Albertan living and writing in British Columbia, George Ryga. Unlike poets and novelists, however, a playwright cannot develop in a vacuum, and a play does not really exist until it has been performed.

The major excuse directors have made for not touching Hardin's plays have seldom been on qualitative or aesthetic grounds. They usually cite the large casts and the number of scene changes — the epic size. These plays, they will assert, are too big for their budgets. It is the same old hypocritical double standard. The plays of Shakespeare and Brecht can have as many characters or scene changes as they need, and contemporary plays from London or New York are wonderful just as they are, but Canadian plays — they'd better have just one set and a cast of three, be universal, socially compassionate, full of humanity and funny as hell — all within the same play — or no director in the established and subsidized theatre will even look at them. At the time I was trying to get the Vancouver Playhouse to look at *Esker Mike*, the Company was busy going bankrupt as a result of producing *The Royal Hunt of the Sun*, an extravaganza by the British playwright, Peter Schaffer — with twenty-four scenes and a cast of forty.

Peter Hay
Vancouver, B.C.
May, 1973

*Esker Mike & His Wife, Agiluk* was first performed at the Factory Lab Theatre in Toronto, Ontario, on June 4, 1971, with the following cast:

| | |
|---|---|
| Esker Mike | Booth Harding Savage |
| Agiluk | June M. Keevil |
| William | Russell Case |
| Oolik | Donna Farron |
| 1st Woman | Jeanette Lourim |
| 2nd Woman | Mary Fleming |
| Toomik | Ann de Villiers |
| Minister | William Garrett |
| Minister's Wife | Jacquelyn Jay |
| Administrator | Carl Gall |
| Priest | James Irving |
| Constable | David Friedman |
| Sgt. Green | Howard Cronis |
| Minister of Northern Affairs | Ashleigh Moorhouse |
| Albert Onchuk | Ashleigh Moorhouse |

Directed by Maruti Achanta
Costumes by Shawn Kerwin
Lighting Design by Peter Ottenhoff

*Esker Mike & His Wife, Agiluk* was also performed by Troupe at Intermedia Hall in Vancouver, British Columbia, on February 3, 1972, with the following cast:

| | |
|---|---|
| Esker Mike | David Petersen |
| Agiluk | B.J. Gordon |
| William | Alexander Diakun |
| Oolik | Mazie Hoy |
| 1st Woman | Sharon Kirk |
| 2nd Woman | Janet Bickford |
| Toomik | Jackie Crossland |
| Minister | Rudy LaValle |
| Minister's Wife | Sharon Kirk |
| Administrator | John Lazarus |
| Priest | Thomas Hauff |
| Constable | Rudy LaValle |
| Sgt. Green | Richard Sutherland |
| Minister of Northern Affairs | Robert Graham |
| Albert Onchuk | Thomas Hauff |

Directed by Jon Bankson
Sets Designed by Mariascha Kalensky
Costumes by Janet Bickford
Lighting Design by Terry Maclean

*Esker Mike & His Wife, Agiluk* was also performed at the Factory Lab Theatre in Toronto, Ontario, on October 26, 1972, with the following cast:

| | |
|---|---|
| Esker Mike | Neil Vipond |
| Agiluk | Carole Zorro |
| William | Dean Hawes |
| Oolik | Maureen McRae |
| 1st Woman | Esther Bogyo |
| 2nd Woman | Margaret Keith |
| Toomik | Doris Petrie |
| Minister | Alexander McLean |
| Minister's Wife | Marietta O'Born |
| Administrator | David Bolt |
| Priest | Peter Kunder |
| Constable | Peter Kunder |
| Sgt. Green | David Fox |
| Minister of Northern Affairs | Keith Mills |
| Albert Onchuk | Steven Whistance-Smith |

Directed by Eric Steiner
Sets Designed by Doug Robinson
Costumes by Sharon Kerwin
Lighting Designed by John Jorgensen

*Esker Mike & His Wife, Agiluk* was also performed at the Factory Festival of Canadian Plays in London, England, on September 24, 1973, with the following cast:

| | |
|---|---|
| Esker Mike | Neil Vipond |
| Agiluk | Joy Coghill |
| William | Dean Hawes |
| Oolik | Carole Zorro |
| 1st Woman | Brenda Donohue |
| 2nd Woman | Robin Beckwith |
| Toomik | Doris Petrie |
| Minister | Howard Mawson |
| Minister's Wife | Patricia Carroll Brown |
| Administrator | David Bolt |
| Priest | Jim Henshaw |
| Constable | George Bassingthwaighte |
| Sgt. Green | David Fox |
| Minister of Northern Affairs | Don McQuarrie |
| Albert Onchuk | Steven Whistance-Smith |

Directed by Eric Steiner

# In the Shack

*A stove. Esker Mike and William are drinking beer out of bottles. Agiluk is sewing. Esker Mike's grievance is real, and felt strongly, but the conversation is mostly comic exaggeration between friends.*

ESKER MIKE:

This is the truth, the whole truth and nothing but the truth, so help me God. I will now tell you a horrible story. Here I am, Esker Mike, that's fished more credit from the Hudson's Bay Company than any known trapper since A. Mackenzie himself. And Agiluk has decided to stop having children.

WILLIAM:

There are other horrible stories, but that is horrible enough. Our race is going to the dogs.

ESKER MIKE:

It's an old Eskimo law that women who won't bear children are left behind in a thick snowdrift. During a blizzard if possible. But she insists on staying in the shack.

WILLIAM:

I would kick her a few times. I would kick those ideas from the south into the sky.

ESKER MIKE:

*You* can kick her if you want. I can't get close enough to smell her, and that's far away. Do you see that store needle in her hand? Now look at this hole in my arm.

WILLIAM:

It's round and deep like an air hole.

ESKER MIKE:

The next time I try to jump on her, she is going to stick that needle into my neck. Harpooned like an old whale. The end of a man widely known in the Delta.

WILLIAM:

A long time ago you could trade her in for another wife. Like that, she's worthless anyway.

ESKER MIKE:

Worthless? Less than worthless. I couldn't get an old bitch of a wheel dog for her. I couldn't even sell her to the Bay for a pouch of tobacco.

WILLIAM:

Problems. These are new problems, and we won't solve them. My mother and all her mothers were under ten feet of silt in the delta before they came to this problem. Now our women live longer, but the men don't like it so much. An old sled wears well, but an old woman wears out.

ESKER MIKE:

Her head is worn out, but that other part of her isn't.

WILLIAM:

That other part must be good for something.

**ESKER MIKE:**

That other part is good for nothing. The muskrats don't breed fast enough, she says, and if the muskrats don't breed fast, then we don't breed fast.

**WILLIAM:**

That's true. You can rat all spring, until your hands are as raw as his underside, and all you get for it is another winter, and another child, if you happen to live with Agiluk.

**ESKER MIKE:**

I've got enough seed for twenty or thirty myself. This country needs population.

**WILLIAM:**

The barren lands. If the women are barren, the land is barren. And if the women are fertile, the children are barren children. They wander everywhere, and they can't do anything but play. Eight children from Agiluk, and it's no easier to keep alive now than it was after the first one.

**ESKER MIKE:**

I don't let that bother me. I ship them off to Inuvik. If I can ship the oldest four to Inuvik, why can't I ship the next four?

**WILLIAM:**

I don't know.

**ESKER MIKE:**

The more the Anglicans get, the more the Catholics want. And the more the Catholics get the more the Anglicans want. The market for muskrat goes up and down but the demand for children in Inuvik is stable.

**WILLIAM:**

Eight Anglicans, just like that!

ESKER MIKE:

Eight Anglicans? I wouldn't give all my trade to one place. *He empties a box of shells onto the table.* These shells are my kids. Suzy, who came first, is in the Anglican hostel. *He places a shell on one side.* John, number two, who came second, is going to be a Catholic. *He places a shell on the other side, etc.* Then Kinga will be Anglican. And Solomon, the fourth, a Catholic. Or did Igtuk come fourth? Then Solomon will be Anglican. Hmmmmmm......Maybe Igtuk was third. Do you remember the winter that Jacob Jacob lost his foot? So Igtuk will be Anglican, Kinga will be Catholic, Solomon, Anglican, and Alice, Catholic. Or Alice, Anglican and Solomon, Catholic. Anyway, the food is just as good in one place as the other. Between a Catholic omelette and an Anglican omelette there is no difference at all.

WILLIAM:

Inuvik!

ESKER MIKE:

Did you know they heat even their garbage in Inuvik? That's some place.

WILLIAM:

I know that in the hostels the children get a free copy of the Bible *and* a free picture of Jesus Christ.

ESKER MIKE:

They smile at their teachers all day, but since my kids are part white they don't smile all the time.

WILLIAM:

Inuvik is Inuvik. Inuvik is not Aklavik. Aklavik is sinking into the mud.

ESKER MIKE:

Aklavik is a rotten hole. If Agiluk doesn't lie down for me tomorrow, I'm going to wreck this shack and move out. If that stove explodes again, I'm going to trade it in for a good Coleman.

WILLIAM:
>On a night like this we should go outside in the sun and talk about it. Everybody is outside. Why stay in here? *They stand up.*

ESKER MIKE:
>Ten years ago she wouldn't be so stubborn. She used to chink her babies with moss. It holds piss like muskeg. You can't beat moss. Now the government has taught her how to use diapers. It's put ideas into her head.

WILLIAM: *philosophically*
>The only thing to do is to shoot her.

ESKER MIKE:
>If she doesn't change her mind, I'll just give her a good hard whack on the head with a two by four. Native spruce from the banks!

WILLIAM:
>A woman on the other side shot her husband. He didn't kill enough seals. Then she was very lonely. She found a new husband right away. But when there were no seals, he was afraid to go home, and camped by himself. *They laugh.* The administrator told us that story.

ESKER MIKE:
>In the Delta, any woman who keeps her legs closed is asking for it.

WILLIAM:
>My grandfather would shoot her, and I would shoot her. The judge knows the difference between our law and outside law. He's a great man. There would be a big trial. I would see all my relatives and we would have a good time.

ESKER MIKE:

> Lucky for you, William, you're not a white man. I was born in Moosomin, Saskatchewan. They let me eat my blubber raw, but they wouldn't let me do a thing like that. They'd take me to Edmonton and hang me by the neck.

WILLIAM:

> I'd tell them the whole story.

ESKER MIKE:

> What's happening to her, that's what I'd like to know. An Eskimo is only supposed to think a day ahead. She's thinking ahead at least a year. You're not like that, are you?

WILLIAM:

> No, I only think up to the next boat, and in the winter, I don't think of anything at all.

ESKER MIKE:

> That's what I thought. *Aloud.* We're going outside to find a cure for your ailment. But I don't know if I'm going to come back.

> *Exit Esker Mike and William.*

# In the Open

*Oolik and Agiluk.*

OOLIK:
> Agiluk. Agiluk.

AGILUK:
> Oolik. Why are you whispering? It's a warm night and the sun is out.

OOLIK:
> I'm whispering so the men won't hear me. They said you were crazy. If they know I'm here, they'll say I'm crazy too.

AGILUK:
> Why should they say that to you, a young and healthy girl with good thighs and no relatives? A certain one wants your warmth. When the time comes, he won't say that.

OOLIK:
> I have *one* relative.

AGILUK:

Yes, a poor step-sister who lets you live alone in a shack as big as a factor's outhouse. And how I became that step-sister only very old men can tell. Listen to me, Oolik. I know it's warm. Go home and try to sleep. If you can't sleep, come to my place and we'll talk. For a girl who's after a boy with a name, talk is the only thing.

OOLIK:

You should know.

AGILUK:

Why should I know?

OOLIK:

If you don't know why, then ask somebody. You can ask the Reverend Smith's little boy and he'll tell you. Esker Mike! Esker Mike and three before him. And now you don't want any more. I won't do it like that.

AGILUK:

I did it as I could. Four men and ten children. Eight are still living. I bore them all without so much as a bloodied hand from the father. And I'm bearing still. A woman's work! Esker Mike knows I'm a woman. But no more children. No more children from Agiluk until a man knows what he is. A seal that slips out of his hole and can't get back in!

OOLIK:

Agiluk!

AGILUK:

When Esker Mike can feed us, then that hole will open up again. Why should my children go to Inuvik? I want them to eat out of their own hands. Nobody's to blame, but I can wait.

OOLIK:

You can wait. Crazy whore! Crazy whore!

AGILUK:

Who said that?

OOLIK:

Esker Mike said that. The men were laughing. They laugh like ghosts, but I can feel that laugh going right through my dress.

AGILUK:

Let them say what they want. If the trapping's no good, they have to talk like that. And women are supposed to keep quiet. You live here and you die here and that's all. Aklavik is a man.

OOLIK:

Aklavik is a white man.

AGILUK:

I took the first one who wasn't afraid of me, and he was white. That's how it was.

OOLIK:

Ooof! I pity your children.

AGILUK:

*I* pity my children.

OOLIK:

You're no mother!

AGILUK:

*My* mother was no mother.

OOLIK:

To bear a wolverine like you!

AGILUK:

A wolverine! She was going to kill me. One girl too many in the camp was like excrement. A bad smell in the tent. But the mission said it was wrong. And after a few days it was impossible. I'm no mother like that. When the time comes, I'll know how to do it.

OOLIK:

     Stay there. You frighten me. I didn't know you were like that.

AGILUK:

     How am I like that?

OOLIK:

     Goodbye.

AGILUK:

     Then you're not coming to my place.

OOLIK:

     Esker Mike is coming to your place and I don't want to be there. I don't want to see what's going to happen.

AGILUK:

     You go home to sleep. What do you know about men, my little Oolik? They can't bring in enough furs. Or they can't get a good price. They go for welfare. On long days like this they like to do something and the women like to do it with them. It's an ordinary thing. But nothing's going to happen to Agiluk.

OOLIK:

     I won't be there anyway.

AGILUK:

     If someone decides the days are too long and takes you home from the hall, why bother waiting? There is only one Agiluk, and if she weakens, she will make herself pay for it.

OOLIK:

     I don't know what you mean. Why don't you talk like everybody else? *Exit Oolik.*

AGILUK:

No more children from Agiluk! *She looks into the sun.* Esker Mike is somewhere and wide awake. Maybe I'll sleep and maybe I won't.

# The Aklavik Fur Co-operative

*Two Women sewing outside.*

FIRST WOMAN:
It's a good thing they didn't wreck the churches and go away to Inuvik. Otherwise Esker Mike and Agiluk would be married in the bush.

SECOND WOMAN:
I was married in a bed of packed snow. It's all the same in the end.

FIRST WOMAN:
All the same? How can you say that? The Anglican Church in the summer has a nice mustiness. It's a real church smell. You don't get that in winter. All you get is the stink of fuel oil.

SECOND WOMAN:
When I married, the only stink I wanted to smell was my husband's.

FIRST WOMAN:
　You must have smelled him all right.

SECOND WOMAN:
　I did, and it was the heavy smell of a man. Even when he was out, I could lie under it.

FIRST WOMAN:
　Yes, if you pressed that smell into a bag, it would fall through thick ice.

SECOND WOMAN:
　A sod house kept smells. Living in a shack is different. There's more room, but it's lonelier.

*They work silently.*

FIRST WOMAN:
　Esker Mike was going to beat her, but marriage is easier than beating Agiluk. There'll be a big crowd today to see what happens.

SECOND WOMAN:
　Not as big as it could be. Summer is a poor season for the church.

FIRST WOMAN:
　It's a good time for weddings. The bride doesn't have to wear leggings underneath her dress.

SECOND WOMAN:
　All things considered, the winter is the best time for Christianity. It's long and dark and bitter, and a man is willing to listen to gloomy stories. In the summer, the crucifixion makes me want to vomit.

FIRST WOMAN:　*looking around*
　Shhhhh! If the Reverend Smith hears you, he'll invite you to tea. You know what that means.

SECOND WOMAN:
>Winter!  That's when Christianity comes in handy. Why shouldn't I say it?  If you're stuck in a tent during a blizzard, you can sing hymns.  It helps to pass the time.

FIRST WOMAN:
>The flying Methodist from Texas always came in summer.

SECOND WOMAN:
>He was a fool.  You can't convert an Eskimo in summer.  It's too light.  A man isn't inclined to stay put.

FIRST WOMAN:
>He converted Imluk last summer.  They carried him into the Great River and that was it.  A Methodist!

SECOND WOMAN:
>Old Imluk thought he was going to walk again!

FIRST WOMAN:
>He came out blue all over, but his legs were still dead. He didn't have enough faith.

SECOND WOMAN:
>He didn't make the grade.

FIRST WOMAN:
>It wasn't long before he was dead.

SECOND WOMAN:
>Our only Methodist!  And how many others are there now in Aklavik?  None.  That's how we are.  If the man from Texas had stayed a winter, he would have had much better results.  Making a good convert is like making a good carving.  When the bone is hard, you have to hack away for a long time.

>*Enter Toomik.*

FIRST WOMAN:

Hello, Toomik. Aren't you going to the wedding?
It's not every day the Anglican Church has something
on in summer.

TOOMIK:

A church to bind Agiluk to Esker Mike? Pah!
There's no church like that! I'm going to meet the
boat.

FIRST WOMAN:

The boat won't be here for a week at least. And the
wedding's today.

TOOMIK:

I'm going to meet the boat. The Christianity will
come and go but the boat will arrive always. Have
you got a cigar?

FIRST WOMAN:

What would we be doing with a cigar?

TOOMIK:

If you had a cigar, I could tell you a thing or two
about Agiluk and her struggle with the spirits. That
struggle will come to a head.....sometime. Maybe
today. Maybe tomorrow. It's too bad you don't
have a cigar.

*Exit Toomik.*

SECOND WOMAN: *singing*

You have lice.
You have lice.

FIRST WOMAN:

Be quiet!

SECOND WOMAN: *continuing*

Some so big you must kill them with a rock.

*She laughs.*

FIRST WOMAN:
>Maybe today. Maybe tomorrow. What did she mean by that?

SECOND WOMAN:
>It was the first thing that came into her head. She wants a cigar, that's all.

FIRST WOMAN:
>I wouldn't say that out loud. Anybody who speaks against Toomik is headed for misfortune.

SECOND WOMAN: *as loud as she can*
>Toomik steals cigars......

FIRST WOMAN:
>Shhhh!

SECOND WOMAN:
>.....and sticks the butts in between her loose floorboards.

FIRST WOMAN: *shocked*
>Sit down. You're lucky if she didn't hear you. Imluk laughed at her, and the bear mangled his legs. She could have given them life, but she didn't.

SECOND WOMAN:
>She could have turned him into a goose with a stench like that. She washes her hair in urine. It used to be the style in her day.

FIRST WOMAN:
>Hold your tongue! Soon it won't be safe to sit with you.

SECOND WOMAN: *screaming*
>The demons!

>*She pricks the First Woman in the behind with her needle.*

FIRST WOMAN:    *jumping up*
Hooo!  The demons!

> *The Second Woman, choking with laughter, holds up the needle.*

I wouldn't be surprised if Toomik had a curse on you right now.

> *The laughter redoubles.*

I don't think it's wise to go to the wedding after all.

> *The laughter continues.*

# Outside the Anglican Church

*Wooden folding chairs. Enter Toomik from one side. Vigorous singing of "O God Our Help In Ages Past" from the other side, offstage. Then enter from that side Esker Mike and Agiluk, and the congregation of Reverend Smith Mrs. Smith, Sergeant Green, the Administrator, Father Roget, Oolik, William and the Second Woman, sprinkling confetti on the couple.*

ESKER MIKE:

This is a fine wedding. A wedding as it should be, by God! Only suits and ties here.

MRS. SMITH:

That was very nice, Mike. You did well. And you did *right*. A good example for some other squatters.

ESKER MIKE:

You can't blame them. They think you're here just to convert Eskimos. They don't know any better.

MRS. SMITH:

    That's it.  But marriage isn't an everyday affair.  You do it once, and it's done.  Now, Sergeant Green, will you take the photographs, please?

OTHERS:

    Photographs!

SGT. GREEN:    *good-naturedly*

    When wasn't I church photographer?  Compared to pulling out an abcessed molar in sub-zero weather, this is humiliating.  But I do it just the same.

ESKER MIKE:

    Photographs?  Good, I want this marriage to be absolutely legitimate.

MRS. SMITH:

    First the bride and groom.

REV. SMITH:

    After eight children!  If you wait long enough in the North, something is bound to happen.

    *Sergeant Green takes a photograph.*

    *Scattered applause.*

SGT. GREEN:

    One more.

MRS. SMITH:

    Beautiful!  The fruits of isolation!  There is nothing like an Anglican wedding on a warm summer day to make one love the North and hate the South.

    *Another photo.*

    *More applause.*

MRS. SMITH:

Now with the best man and the bridesmaid.

*William and Oolik arrange themselves.*

*Photograph.*

*Applause.*

Now everyone, please. Is that all right, Sergeant Green? Come along, Father Roget.

*Photograph.*

*Conviviality.*

ESKER MIKE: *aloud to William*

I'm glad that's over. Now Agiluk will have to sleep with me whether she likes it or not.

MRS. SMITH:
Mike!

REV. SMITH: *considerately*

That's the old North talking. We're trying to make a new North in the church.

ESKER MIKE:
What? Holy and legal southern wedlock! You said it today and you said it yesterday.

FATHER ROGET: *to the Administrator*
Anglican wedlock, in this case.

MRS. SMITH:
He's got his nerve.

ESKER MIKE:

Fortunately, today I *am* an Anglican. Why else would I come to an Anglican Church? When I want a church it is always the Anglican Church I come to first, if it's open.

*Murmurings from crowd.*

ESKER MIKE:

The marriage ceremony fixes it like a hook in a fish.

*More reaction.*

REV. SMITH:

We can talk about this in the rectory.

ESKER MIKE:

You can do your dirty work in the rectory. I'm going to kick my children out for the afternoon and show my wife what a man I am!

REV. SMITH:

We're all men here. The great ones suffer the loneliness and the weak ones cannot. The fact that you have something between your legs will not impress her at all.

MRS. SMITH:

Harold, what have you said?

REV. SMITH:

Yes, I said it. And now I'm going to sit down.

ESKER MIKE:

Look at that, William. The Anglican Church is sitting in a chair. I could knock it over with the back of my foot.

MRS. SMITH:

>You wouldn't dare.

ESKER MIKE:

>I wouldn't dirty my good pair of boots. The church is rotting anyway. You can see it with your own eyes.

REV. SMITH:

>You can leave the grounds right now.

ESKER MIKE:

>I'll leave when I want. There's no place in the Delta where a man can't stop if he wants to.

>>*Sergeant Green signals negatively with his head.*

>Well, I'll go in a minute. We still have to celebrate. Ten years with Agiluk and then I married her. For Aklavik, that's a record.

TOOMIK:

>A marriage that does everything undoes everything!

ESKER MIKE:

>Listen to that. The ties in a Christian marriage are stronger than the spring in a No. 8 trap.

AGILUK:

>I am not a Christian.   *She begins to undress.*

MRS. SMITH:

>What are you doing, woman?

AGILUK:

I am taking off this dress. I wore it to please you but I don't want to wear it any more. *She removes it. Underneath are her regular clothes.* I am not a virgin, and I don't believe in them either. I can only believe in myself, which is nothing. So I don't believe in anything at all.

*Mrs. Smith snatches away the dress.*

*Exit Agiluk.*

TOOMIK:

The marriage is dead, phttt, like an Arctic crocus. It should last longer, but it's gone before you know it.

ESKER MIKE:

What's that?

TOOMIK:

You have to be a Christian husband now, but Agiluk will be Agiluk. *She chuckles.* Agiluk! Agiluk!

ESKER MIKE: *to Reverend Smith*

You got me into this. Now you can get me out of it.

REV. SMITH:

Go home. I can't do anything today.

ESKER MIKE:

You wouldn't leave me married to a disbeliever. I'd go to hell, wouldn't I? You should give me an annulment.

REV. SMITH:

Ten minutes after the wedding?

ESKER MIKE:

> An annulment is good anytime. I want one quick. On the grounds that my wife refuses to consume the marriage.

REV. SMITH:

> Not on those grounds. Not after all the children.

ESKER MIKE:

> If you can't give me an annulment, then Father Roget will give me an annulment.

ADMINISTRATOR:     *to himself*

> The Anglicans bind and the Catholics cleave.

ESKER MIKE:

> These priests around here can do anything. Father McGeorge and his tug! Two blasts from his whistle and you knew that Christ was on his way with the Maple Leaf lard and the nails.

REV. SMITH:

> I won't compete. This is senseless.

FATHER ROGET:

> It would be out of place for me....a guest....

MRS. SMITH:

> Certainly out of place!

FATHER ROGET:

> I'm not in a position. This is Anglican territory. In Fort Simpson it would be different.

> *Mrs. Smith hisses quietly.*

> *The crowd is embarrassed.*

ESKER MIKE:
>That's a nice story. Do they give annulments in Fort Simpson? What's wrong with Aklavik?

FATHER ROGET:
>In the circumstances....I can only tell you what possibilities the church offers. *He starts out seriously, but grows progressively angry at himself as he becomes aware of how inappropriate and futile his speech is.* To begin with, if one spouse refuses to have children, then the other has certain grounds.... On the other hand, Agiluk has mothered eight children and has chosen abstinence, a very Catholic measure. Catholic without knowing it. That's how Eskimos are. A wonderful people. Yes, that's true. On the other hand, all eight children are illegitimate, and two of them by other men. Then four are Anglican. Which should count in our considerations? All eight of them, illegitimate, the six by Esker Mike, the four Catholic children only, the three Catholic children by Esker Mike, or none of them. That is a question which the Rota of the Vatican must decide. On the other hand, a marriage outside the church can't be considered a marriage, so we might be applying for the annulment of a marriage which doesn't exist. *Bitterly.* Well, it's all useless! It doesn't fit! *Trying again calmly.* In any case, these things take time.

ESKER MIKE:
>How much time? The Bay sells traps across the counter. Why should I wait for an annulment? Annulments in the South, but crosses in the North! You can never get what you want without paying too high a price. Cabbage, sixty-one cents a pound!

MRS. SMITH: *weeping*
>This is terrible.

ESKER MIKE:
> I'm not a Christian anyway.

REV. SMITH:
> For the last time, get out.

ESKER MIKE:
> That church smells. You use too much disinfectant.
> The next time I want a church, I'll give Toomik a box
> of cigars.

> *Exit Esker Mike.*

TOOMIK:     *calling*
> Wait for me! Wait for old Toomik!     *She stumbles.*
> Ouch! Priests and hungry owls! Hey!

> *Exit Toomik, hobbling.*

MRS. SMITH:
> This is terrible. I hate it! I hate all of this!

> *Exit Mrs. Smith.*

# Main Street

*The Minister of Northern Affairs and the Administrator, followed in a straight line by Reverend Smith, Sergeant Green and Constable MacIntyre. Also the Townspeople, including Agiluk, somewhat apart.*

ADMINISTRATOR:    *sardonically*
I told him he should move to Inuvik, and he began to weep.

MINISTER:
My God!  You've got to be damned careful with these people.

ADMINISTRATOR:
Free land, I said, and a 512 for four thousand dollars. And all he did was sit there and look at me.  In his case, we can't even get the horse to water.

MINISTER:

> The same as two years ago. And seven years ago! We're spending millions in the Delta! How do they do it in Norilsk? The Danish ambassador told me he can't make head nor tail of this place. All civilized men, he said, and nothing's civilized. What a contradiction! Greenland was never like this.

ADMINISTRATOR: *sceptically*

> The Danish ambassador? They say a Greenlander will study the Bible, but an Inuk will skin it. The Delta is its *own* civilization.

MINISTER:

> I didn't appreciate that. Stop talking in riddles. I thought I could count on my own men, at least, to explain the situation. There's something here I can't quite grasp, some central fact which eludes all of us, that if we could only seize upon.....

ADMINISTRATOR:

> There's no solution. Why should there be?

MINISTER:

> I never thought of that. *He reflects.* No. It's impossible. It defies common sense. You gave me a start.

> *They stroll on.*

ADMINISTRATOR:

> What does H.B.C. stand for?

MINISTER: *incredulous*

> Hudson's Bay Company!

ADMINISTRATOR:
Here Before Christ.

*The Minister smiles and nods his head.*

What time do you think it is?

MINISTER: *looking at the sky*
I seem to have lost all sense.... You can't tell on days like this, can you?

ADMINISTRATOR:
No you can't. A day like any other day.

MINISTER:
There you go. Conundrums again!

ADMINISTRATOR:
The sun stays out all day, so the words come out of my mouth like flies out of a jar.

MINISTER:
This is depressing. I've been depressed ever since Tuktoyaktuk. They gave me a banquet of muktuk and I had to eat the stuff. My metabolism's shot to hell!

ADMINISTRATOR:
The same thing happened to Canarvy and he ate chocolate bars. He ended up trying to walk to White-horse.

MINISTER:
Are you pulling my leg? Listen, it sounds silly, but the worst part is not knowing when to eat lunch. How can I think about rot and poverty? I keep on thinking about myself. *He stops.* This is en-demic, isn't it? I'm not the only one?

ADMINISTRATOR:
> No. I keep on thinking that history never happened.
> Julius Caesar was a muskrat! Or that the world is in
> the shape of a skullcap. Step below the Circle and
> you fall into space.

MINISTER:
> My God! What's that got to do with it?    *Con-
> scientiously.*    Capital investment!  Transport!
> Wage opportunities!  Let's get down to earth.  Can
> we or can we not bring these things to the Delta?
> The Russians are twenty years ahead!  Let's at least
> find out what the people feel!

> *He greets Agiluk.*

> Good morning.

ADMINISTRATOR:
> Agiluk.  The Minister of Northern Affairs.

> *The other Townspeople come nearer.  The
> Minister offers his hand.  Agiluk stares.  He
> bends forward as if to offer his nose.  She
> impulsively bites it.  He shrieks. Constable Mac-
> Intyre seizes her.*

MINISTER:
> No!  Let her go!

> *Agiluk is freed and leaves.*

> Blood!  What does it mean?    Is this some kind of
> primitive ritual?  Why didn't you warn me?

ADMINISTRATOR:
> Yes, why didn't I?  Maybe I should have warned *her.*

MINISTER:
> I'm still bleeding. Thanks a lot. I've heard of rubbing noses, but biting noses.... It's not humiliating. It's saddening. Sad! Sad! *He turns to the Administrator.* What was her name?

ADMINISTRATOR:
> Agiluk.

MINISTER: *distracted*
> Agiluk. Her eyes. Those were winter eyes and it's midsummer. My God! Our master plan for the District seems so far away now.

> *Exit the Minister and the Administrator, followed in a line by Reverend Smith, Sergeant Green and Constable MacIntyre.*

# The Administrator's Office

*William and Esker Mike.*

ESKER MIKE:
> Down at the mouth! Are you sure you weren't a whale once? If you look like that when he comes in, he'll grow suspicious and make me fill out forms.

WILLIAM:
> Maybe I should go home.

ESKER MIKE:
> Go home? A friend like you wouldn't go home.

WILLIAM:
> I'm sad today.

ESKER MIKE:
> You still can't go home. With you here, he might mistake me for a white-faced Eskimo. A bastard. It runs in the family.

WILLIAM:

> Bastards look like everybody else.

ESKER MIKE:

> They're not like everybody else, though. The illegitimate kind are much better than the others when it comes to welfare. My children get extra candy at Inuvik. *By way of explanation.* Bastards.

> *William examines Esker Mike.*

WILLIAM:

> You can't be an Eskimo. You have to shave every day.

ESKER MIKE:

> It's the atmosphere. If he feels there are Eskimos around, he won't be so mean. *He rubs his chin.* It is rough. Well, I'm not going to pluck them out. There's a limit.

WILLIAM:

> If you *were* an Eskimo, you could make a good living telling stories. Before, there were no storytellers. Only people who told stories. Now we can sell them like furs.

ESKER MIKE:

> That's a racket for you! I'm only going to borrow some money from the government.

WILLIAM:

> Yes, I'm sad today, sadder than I've been for a long while.

ESKER MIKE:

> Oh, you know how to be sad all the time.

**WILLIAM:**

But now I'm weeping for Esker Mike, who will soon be gone. Neytuna invented a cousin too. And the Administrator killed him. Ah, Neytuna! He realized he had done wrong! "I'm miserable," he used to cry. "But now that I have this cousin, what can I do with him?"

**ESKER MIKE:**

He could have abandoned him to the weather.

**WILLIAM:**

No, he couldn't. The Administrator wouldn't allow it. He kept on giving Neytuna money for his cousin until Neytuna died from misery. It was a punishment that even Toomik couldn't have thought of. Slow, like starvation, but with no hunger.

**ESKER MIKE:**

What a story! The Administrator is as simple as cold.

**WILLIAM:**  *contemplatively*

No. He can smell evil at five hundred yards, whichever way the wind is blowing.

**ESKER MIKE:**

You're an underdeveloped native, William. He can't smell a dead char when it's five days old. A man who sits in a chair inside a heated house can't smell anything.

**WILLIAM:**

I don't care about the char. He can smell evil inside an oil drum.

ESKER MIKE:

> Since I don't believe in your disgusting old demons, and since I'm a pioneer in good standing, I'm going to ask him for the money anyway. It's only the grubstake. The profit comes by itself. Esker Mike and Company and Sons Ltd.... that's about it. When Agiluk sees me holding a Chamber of Commerce in the Native Hall, she'll decide we can risk another offspring after all.

WILLIAM:

> This is worse than waiting for a vaccination.

ESKER MIKE:

> It will all be over in ten minutes. You just have to teach me how you do it.

WILLIAM:

> I stand in line.

ESKER MIKE:

> Is that all?

WILLIAM:

> And then he looks me in the eye, and I just stand there.

ESKER MIKE:

> You're no Eskimo. I can do better than that. You have to grin. Otherwise he thinks you're up to no good.

WILLIAM:

> I just stand in front of him, like this.    *He stands, a proud man beggared.*

**ESKER MIKE:**

No, you have to grin. And pretend you're shy. It helps if your teeth are yellow.

*He strikes a pose. Enter the Administrator, who eventually looks up.*

**ADMINISTRATOR:**

Is that an abcessed bicuspid? In the old days Sergeant Green would have them all out in an afternoon.

*Esker Mike points to the gaps in his teeth.*

**ESKER MIKE:**

As a matter of fact, this one is lying in Sergeant Green's cupboard, next to a killer bullet and other important souvenirs of his lifetime. This one was swallowed by my lead dog Mabel, who then began to slobber, and died from infection.

**WILLIAM:**

These young constables who can't pull teeth aren't worth spitting at.

**ESKER MIKE:**

This has nothing to do with welfare, but can I show William your molars?

*The Administrator sits down and opens his mouth.*

See. Perfect. I told you, William.

**WILLIAM:**

I've seen better. How about Miss Reynolds, the teacher? *Her* teeth were perfect. Full of gold! Whenever she was hungry, she could get credit just by opening her mouth.

50

*The Administrator opens a file.*

ADMINISTRATOR:     *reading*
>    Esker Mike.     *He peruses the contents.*    This is one
>    of the best welfare portfolios I've worked out in my
>    life, if not *the* best.    Well-balanced security at all
>    times and all seasons. I don't think the Prime Minister
>    himself could manage to give you more money.

ESKER MIKE:
>    Oh, the Prime Minister.   He's not an Arctic linguist
>    and scholar like you.

ADMINISTRATOR:
>    Neither is Sergeant Green.   If I gave you the beaver
>    off a nickel, I'd be in prison tomorrow.

ESKER MIKE:     *chastened*
>    Prison?

WILLIAM:
>    How can the government send itself to prison?

ESKER MIKE:     *philosophically*
>    The government can do what it wants.   They could
>    put old Tulugak on a stick and roast him to a crisp.

WILLIAM:
>    Nobody could do that to Tulugak.   He'd turn into a
>    grain of sand.   He was a spirit!

ESKER MIKE:
>    A spirit?   Don't give us that.   Tulugak was a son-of-a-
>    bitch.   A raven who did it to women!   You couldn't
>    run a Sunday School with stories like that.   The
>    government would censor you into the ground.

ADMINISTRATOR:
>  Sodomy with huskies and young caribou is also dis-
>  couraged.

ESKER MIKE:  *uneasy*
>  I'm not a caribou man myself.

ADMINISTRATOR:  *musing*
>  Entry from the rear.  The South enters the North
>  from the rear.  Sodomy as it should be done, in
>  Canada as it is in the U.S.  *He smiles at his own
>  humour.*  Opening up the territories!  *To Esker
>  Mike.*  When they open up the territories, where are
>  you going to go?  Any further north, and you'd soon
>  be heading south.  The Sisyphus of the Arctic wastes!
>  Esker Mike versus the shape of the earth!

ESKER MIKE:  *alarmed*
>  I don't know where I'd go!  I'm North wherever I am!

ADMINISTRATOR:  *cynically nodding his head*
>  The tragic archetype of the 67th parallel!  *He
>  looks intently at Esker Mike.*  What a discovery!
>  I see the Ancient Mariner in his Stanfield thermal
>  underwear, damned to float endlessly downstream a-
>  stride a forty-gallon drum!

>  *Esker Mike first looks behind him.*

ESKER MIKE:  *puzzled*
>  He sounds hungry and cold.  *Awkwardly.*  He
>  sounds almost as hungry as Agiluk's cousin, who is so
>  desperate that a mere look from her good eye could
>  melt a frozen dog from your door and turn him into
>  mock muktuk.

ADMINISTRATOR:  *cunningly*
>  Agiluk's cousin?  Where did she come from?

ESKER MIKE:

    She's from one of the ten lost tribes.

ADMINISTRATOR:

    Ten lost tribes?  Biblical fairy tales!  Mediterranean scum!

ESKER MIKE:

    I mean, she just came from nowhere, from some tent somewhere out there.  From out of the great space!

ADMINISTRATOR: *amused*

    And you intended to let her starve.  That's why you didn't come to me.  Otherwise you would have come to me.

ESKER MIKE:

    But...

ADMINISTRATOR:

    The strong dispose of the feeble.  A fine tradition revived.  Only these days it happens to be murder!

ESKER MIKE:

    But.... I mean.... She doesn't exist!  I just made her up!

ADMINISTRATOR: *severely*

    Let's have the truth.  You would look her in the face until that face couldn't look back!

ESKER MIKE:

    No!  It wasn't me!  It was Agiluk!  She's a primitive one, you know.  The spitting image of her great, great grandmother, who still comes to see her, in the shape of a dog or a lynx.  Do you want to hear that story?

    *The Administrator looks at him, then opens a drawer with a key.*

ADMINISTRATOR:

Here's forty dollars for this month. But I don't want to see how she looks at you. Keep her healthy, but keep her out of my sight.

*Esker Mike and William rise.*

ESKER MIKE:

Oh, you won't see her. I'll take care of that. You don't have to worry about that.

*Exit Esker Mike and William.*

ADMINISTRATOR:

Agiluk's cousin?

*He laughs diabolically.*

*Exit.*

# Main Street

*Sergeant Green and Esker Mike.*

SGT. GREEN:
> Hey! Where are you running to, you toothless mistake for a polar bear?

ESKER MIKE:
> If I were a bear, I wouldn't have to use my teeth. I'd just knock off your head with my paw, in one swoop.

SGT. GREEN:
> A policeman's head?

ESKER MIKE:
> It would come off like moss from a stone, Sergeant. A man tears easy, though you'll have to ask Elijah how he tastes. That's one winter he won't forget.

SGT. GREEN:
> It was a long time ago.

ESKER MIKE:

It wouldn't happen now, would it? Nobody gets lost and stranded now in midwinter. We just radio Inuvik and ask for an airplane or two.

SGT. GREEN:

It was his boots or his brother-in-law. So he decided to eat his brother-in-law. And we didn't even arrest him. Why bother the Magistrate with a family affair?

ESKER MIKE:

Do you see how calm and warm it is today? It's so warm I can see that spruce tree growing. Sad talk makes me tremble on a warm day like this.

SGT. GREEN:

Is that why you were running?

ESKER MIKE:

I wasn't running. I was walking fast.

SGT. GREEN:

Nobody runs here. Running is suicide. It freezes the lungs. Or it fills them with flies. Only fugitives run in Aklavik. When I see somebody running, I chase him.

ESKER MIKE:

You don't have to chase me, Sergeant.

SGT. GREEN:

If I don't chase you today, I chase you tomorrow.

ESKER MIKE:

What do you mean?

SGT. GREEN:

Can't you feel it in your bones? Aklavik is no place for a man who wants to get ahead like you. You didn't trap enough muskrat this season to chink the drafts in your shack.

ESKER MIKE:

I must be growing weak. It's the harsh climate.

SGT. GREEN:

And you're an old fornicator. You've got all those little mouths to feed.

ESKER MIKE:

That's true enough. I find women suitable. I've been fornicating for the best part of my life.

SGT. GREEN:

So sooner or later, you're going to try to cheat the government. It follows, doesn't it?

ESKER MIKE:

Yes, it follows. Can I stop it from following?

SGT. GREEN:

I wouldn't be surprised if you invented a new relative just to collect more welfare on her behalf.

ESKER MIKE:     *waking*

Why would I do a thing like that?

SGT. GREEN:

I just told you why. And when I come to arrest you, you'll know the reason.     *He pulls an old pair of handcuffs out of his pocket.*     Do you see these cuffs?

ESKER MIKE:

The cuffs?  You'd better save those for a criminal like Constable Mac who arrests men for nothing at all. Goodbye, Sergeant.  I wouldn't do anything wrong. I was just running to meet the boat.  The first mate and I are going to make a business deal and become as rich as store clerks.  You'll never have to arrest me. I think clean thoughts and do good deeds, every day and in every way.  *He hurries away.*  The government!  I'd better find a cousin somewhere or I'm in for it.

*Exit Esker Mike.*

*Sergeant Green laughs.*

SGT. GREEN:

Look at that dismal specimen of mankind.  A true son of the North!  Well, one extra cousin isn't so bad. But if he puts another on the list, I'll have to threaten him with a trip to the Outside.  *He smiles.*  The Outside!  He'd rather be skinned and hung out to dry on a willow frame.

# The Mate's Cabin

*Albert and William at a table.*

*Enter Esker Mike.*

ESKER MIKE:
What do I see?　A Hay River rat who's come down North for air!

ALBERT:
Air?　That's about all.　Hay River for me!　Lots of tables in the beer parlour.　A road to the Peace.　And French fries in a box.

ESKER MIKE:
I don't see what's so good about that. You live with an Indian woman in Hay River and they call you a squaw man.

ALBERT:

Calm down. Relax. I didn't call you a squaw man. God, you people in Aklavik are crazy. Always growling. What's wrong? Can't you keep alive here? *He grins.* When a white man crosses the Arctic Circle, he changes into another man. You wouldn't know him.

ESKER MIKE:

The Arctic Circle's only a line in the air.

ALBERT:

I can't say how it happens. Once I told a tourist he was crossing. He looked at me for a while, and then he fainted.

ESKER MIKE: *laughing*

Stupid! Those tourists are stupid! *He sits down.*

ALBERT:

William and I thought you caught your finger in a trap, so we opened the merchandise.

ESKER MIKE: *furious*

You opened it?

> *Albert and William laugh. Albert produces an unopened bottle.*

ALBERT:

Made from fine rye grain and Rocky Mountain water. Nine ninety-five. Here's your nickel change. Albert Onchuk's as honest as the day is long.

ESKER MIKE:

As the day is long in December, maybe. *He pulls out an old list.* The price here is five forty-five.

60

ALBERT:

That's in Alberta. This is Aklavik. One thousand miles by water from Fort Providence. You have to pay for your liquor F.O.B. Aklavik!

ESKER MIKE:

Four dollars to put this bottle in your bag? Shit! I could get it cheaper from Inuvik.

ALBERT:

It's not the weight you're paying for, it's the discomfort. Insects! When we stopped at Wrigley, the flies were half an inch thick on the deck. You couldn't see white. We had to shovel them off.

ESKER MIKE:

Those aren't flies. We have flies here that can black out a lantern at dead of night, in five seconds flat! That hunter from New York didn't have a chance.

ALBERT: *suspiciously*
What hunter?

ESKER MIKE:

He marked his tent with an oil lamp when he stepped outside to pee. And he *never* found his way back.

ALBERT: *with deliberation*
Three hundred miles upriver, I killed a mosquito as big as my thumb. A jiggerful of Albert Onchuk's blood! I could have had him stuffed. but he was squashed flat.

ESKER MIKE:

Ha! I've seen mosquitoes make a man's skin puff like a balloon and kill him with fever. Our Aklavik flies drove Mr. Catack crazy. Now he can walk through a swarm stark naked and come out with no sores at all, but plenty of flies in his mouth. He eats so many flies he doesn't have to eat meat.

ALBERT:

> Liar!

> *Esker Mike grabs Albert by the shirt.*

ESKER MIKE:

> You little runt. If worse things don't happen to us every day then the North is the South, and the South is the North.

ALBERT:

> Okay.

ESKER MIKE:

> And what about that four and a half dollars you robbed me of?

ALBERT:

> Okay. Okay.

> *Albert hands over the money.*

> I'm doing this because you're my business partner. What took you so long? I thought you'd be the first one here.

ESKER MIKE:

> I was paying my respects to the law, in the person of Sergeant Green.

ALBERT:

> The whole town went through this boat in fifteen minutes.

ESKER MIKE:

> If there was a boat every day, they would drop dead from excitement. But I wouldn't give my foreskin for the luxury cruise to Arctic Red River.

ALBERT:

On Dominion Day I danced with the Captain. He only knows how to waltz. The men of Fort Norman danced with the men of Fort Norman. We had one woman guest. She was over sixty. Pierre Matoy offered her eighty-five for the night and all he got was a kiss on the cheek.

ESKER MIKE:

We know how to dance. William can do the jig and the two-step. I'm best at the Scottish reel.     *To William.*     Do you mind if Albert takes you around the floor?

WILLIAM:

Practice makes perfect.

ALBERT:

I'm not fussy. Why should I be?

*Esker Mike plays his harmonica.*

*Albert and William dance.*

ESKER MIKE:

Now that I've seen you dancing with a man I don't have to see anything else.

ALBERT:

Forget it. I can pick up a Loucheux woman and forget about it in ten minutes. I'm trying to forget what a backward dump this place is, so we can get down to business.

ESKER MIKE:

Business!     *He pronounces the syllables.*     Business!

ALBERT:
> We'll fleece those tourists until they have to fly South with the ducks.

> *They begin to chuckle, and end by laughing uncontrollably.*

> I'll sign them on at Hay River. The deluxe two-way package tour down and up the Mackenzie! All stops included! Beautiful Norman Wells! Exotic Fort Good Hope! The gay night life of downtown Aklavik!

ESKER MIKE:
> They can sleep in my lean-to at five dollars a time. One dollar extra for hot water. Eggs, fifty cents each!

ALBERT:
> Mosquitoes on the family plan!

ESKER MIKE:
> Muskrat meat à la mode!

ALBERT:
> Just introduce them to a few live Eskimos and they'll go out of their heads. Americans!

ESKER MIKE:
> Americans! They'll make me rich!

> *Grinning.*

> Esker Mike, trapper and capitalist!

ALBERT:
> Capitalism! That's a philosophy!

ESKER MIKE:
> Elijah Kimuit has three washing machines, one mother-in-law and an old schooner. I'm going to buy myself three kickers for my scow and a second-hand carburetor for the stove.

ALBERT:
> Did I hear you say you were a capitalist?  I've been looking at this table, but I don't see any of your capital  yet.

ESKER MIKE:        *suspiciously*
> Capital?  Why don't *you* give me *your* capital? You're supposed to cheat the tourists.  You're not supposed to cheat me.

ALBERT:
> You need a head office to cheat even fat from a grizzly.  And all head offices are in the South.  Don't you know anything about the tourist business?

ESKER MIKE:
> No, but I'm learning fast.        *He leans forward menacingly.*        I'm learning what a fickle partner you are.

ALBERT:        *coldly*
> You can learn lots of things if you want.  Even if you can't read.  You can look at the pictures in the Eaton's catalogue all your life, and become a professor without leaving your shack.  I'll just find somebody else.

ESKER MIKE:
> You're a Hay River rat all right!        *Esker Mike is undecided.  He pauses, then empties a pants pocket and throws the contents on the table.*        There it is! Genuine Canadian dollars, panned from the gold-laden banks of our local river.

ALBERT:

> That's some pan that can separate banknotes from silt and rusty junk, which is all you've got for minerals in this place. *He stares at the table.* I'm not touching crooked money.

ESKER MIKE:

> It's not crooked. It's just welfare for my wife's cousin, who just happens not to exist.

ALBERT:

> And the Administrator is just going to lock us up!

ESKER MIKE:

> Don't worry about him. He's got his mind on other things. He wants me and the ladies in the co-op to take over the Hudson's Bay. I'll be Prime Minister. *Seriously.* If he pokes his nose around, I'll borrow a sister from William. He can't tell one Eskimo from another in broad daylight.

ALBERT:

> That sounds like him. I admit it. *He counts the money.* Not very much. Give me that four dollars in your pocket too.

> *Esker Mike does so.*

> You can keep the half-dollar change.

ESKER MIKE:

> Aren't we supposed to have a contract?

ALBERT:

> A contract? You don't even have a last name.

ESKER MIKE:

> I'm only me. That's how I've always been.

ALBERT:

You can't make a contract legal without a last name. Take my word for it. Now, are we finished? I want to go visit the town, to see if those cabbages are really two feet wide, and anything else of historical importance and scientific wonder.

ESKER MIKE:

I won't stop you from enjoying the pleasures of Aklavik before it's overrun by tourists. William and I will just stay behind in the privacy of your luxurious cabin and celebrate your arrival.

ALBERT:    *rising*

Maybe I'll drop in on your shack and say hello to my old friend Agiluk. With your permission. I know what your rights are now.

ESKER MIKE:

Go ahead. Maybe you can put her back into the habit while you're there.

ALBERT:    *gasping with surprise*
Ah! Maybe I can.

        *Exit Albert.*

WILLIAM:

It's crooked money so it's gone to a crooked man, like sun to summer.

ESKER MIKE:

William, you don't understand how money works. Open a head office and you can step on your neighbour the next day. After that, they'll put you on the council.

WILLIAM:

> You shouldn't dream. Once you start, you can't stop. It's like falling asleep in the snow.

ESKER MIKE:

> *You* dream all the time.

WILLIAM:

> The difference is, I began when I was a boy. One sleep of a dog each day. It takes practice, or you lose control. But now it's as hard as it was at the beginning.

ESKER MIKE:

> William, I could kill you. I'm just inviting you to finish this bottle first. The sound of water underneath this boat makes me think of my unlucky youth, and I don't feel like drinking alone.

# Outside the Boat

TOOMIK: *singing*
>Does Idloo kill the bear?
>Idloo is possessed!   Idloo is possessed!
>He kills it with a sharp laugh.
>
>Does Idloo kill the flood?
>Idloo is possessed!   Idloo is possessed!
>He kills it with a fast boat.
>
>Does Idloo kill the dark?
>Idloo is possessed!   Idloo is possessed!
>He kills it with a great sleep.

ESKER MIKE:
>Hey, Toomik!   What kind of song is that?

TOOMIK:
>It's an old song. Are you the Captain?

ESKER MIKE:   *assuming the Captain's voice*
 Why would an old woman want to know?

TOOMIK:
 That's good.  You sound like Esker Mike, but it's better to be a Captain on an afternoon like this.

ESKER MIKE:
 What do you know about afternoons like this?

TOOMIK:
 I know what comes before night.

ESKER MIKE:
 What else do you know?

TOOMIK:
 I know that your mate is visiting Agiluk and if Esker Mike catches him, he'll shoot him dead.

ESKER MIKE:
 I won't do no such thing.  I would ordinarily, but a man doesn't shoot his own guest.  Maybe I'll shoot you instead.

TOOMIK:
 Do what you want.

ESKER MIKE:
 If he puts a finger on Agiluk, she'll jab it like a small trout.  Why should I shoot him?

TOOMIK:
 Don't ask me.  I can tell you stories of Agiluk's childhood.  I can tell you how she rolled down a hill in a skin when she wasn't much older than her youngest.  But I don't know the answers.  Don't ask me why.

**ESKER MIKE:**

I won't.  I won't even ask you why you're still living, when your teeth are out and you can't see a needle, and when you're going to die anyway.

**TOOMIK:**

Just as well.  If you did, I couldn't answer.  But there will be others before me.  The boat is here and the mate is elsewhere.  This morning I smelled rain in the air.  Don't you know what that means?  You don't, and neither do I.

*Exit Toomik.*

**ESKER MIKE:**     *calling after*
Old witch!  Dried dung of a tern!

# In the Shack

*Agiluk.*

*Albert is drinking tea.*

ALBERT:

Agiluk, Queen of the North! I knew you wouldn't keep an old friend out.

AGILUK:

I wouldn't keep anybody out. This house is as open as no house. Tents have no doors. It's a habit. You could come in at four in the morning. A murderer could come in. I couldn't stop him.

ALBERT:

You couldn't stop a twelve year old boy!

AGILUK:     *scornfully*

Yes, if a man came through that door looking for a lay, he would come through the door. If a bow-legged man I once knew came through that door with a bulge in his pants and asked for tea, I would let him.

ALBERT:

Nothing's changed!

AGILUK:

I would let him wipe out a dirty cup and drink tea from it. That's a man right. You can't refuse his stomach. But if he tried to touch me, I would do something else.

ALBERT:

In the old days, you knew how to do one thing. What else would you do? You still skin your catch on the floor. And the deckhand said you were just as good as I had told him. Good as ever!

AGILUK:

They used to say other things. A man alone on a long river can say what he wants.

ALBERT:

I'll tell you what he said. He said above the Circle there's nothing like it. Eskimo women are always good, I said.

AGILUK:

Here is your man. Here is the snow knife on the table. If that man had a right hand, he was a liar!

ALBERT:

You wild bitch! Wild Agiluk!

AGILUK:

I am....myself. You can run out of here screaming and call for the Sergeant. It will be Agiluk who did it. It was Agiluk who said yes, and Agiluk who is saying no.

ALBERT:

Wild! Wild!

AGILUK:

I have to defend myself. All of Aklavik knows. Why shouldn't I tell you? I am fighting against my unborn children already, just as if they were in me and alive.

ALBERT:

You need a man. If you don't have a man, you'll go right out of your mind.

AGILUK:

A man's conceit! I've had three men and you. Esker Mike is a man!

ALBERT:

He's a man, and he isn't. He stole money from the government and I've got it in my pocket.    *He removes the money.*    It's new enough to break.

*Agiluk stares at the money.*

AGILUK:    *dumbfounded*

The government's money? Esker Mike's money?

ALBERT:

Albert Onchuk's money! Money that's on its way to Hay River, that booming little city on the shores of Great Slave Lake. Or maybe I'll give you a share. I can see you're going downhill. All the women here are fifty years old, even the ones that are just twenty.

74

AGILUK:

> You know where he is?

ALBERT:

> I know where he was.  Underneath a bottle of rye.
> By now he must be underneath the wharf.

AGILUK:

> Underneath the wharf?

ALBERT:

> He's going to slide into the mud like a muskrat, and
> float away.  You can look for him in the Beaufort
> Sea.

AGILUK:

> I'll look for him nowhere.  *Strongly.*  When I am
> gone, Esker Mike can claim his rights with me for
> the last time! Not until then!

ALBERT:  *standing up, horrified*

> What are you talking about?  *He approaches.*
> You're hot!  Look at the sweat on your arms.

AGILUK:

> It's a hot day.

ALBERT:

> It's not that hot.  And the stove is off.

AGILUK:

> It's hot.  The tarpaper brings in the heat.  It loses it
> quickly too.  The walls of this house are like my own
> skin.  *Distractedly.*  I think of what might happen
> and my breasts ache!

ALBERT:

> Breasts like old pelts!

AGILUK:

They served!

ALBERT:

Thighs that could grapple with a bear!

AGILUK:

Yes, all muscle and used to bruises. That's how it's been ever since I remember. *Melancholic.* Thighs like the two banks of our river. Each of my children lay like a winter across me. My belly was thick. Underneath the blood flowed. And then I pushed them out. The river can't stand it anymore, and with a great groan, it opens up and new life shows itself. Ten children! After comes the summer.

ALBERT:

The summer! Those thighs know a tugboat when they see it!

# On the Wharf

*Constable MacIntyre, the Administrator, Esker
Mike, William, Oolik, Toomik, the Two Women.*

CONSTABLE:
How I hate to see that boat go.  I hate to see any boat
go.  The only departure I want to see is my own.

ADMINISTRATOR:
Why think about it?  Nobody leaves Aklavik.

CONSTABLE:  *sullenly*
Are you serious?

ADMINISTRATOR:
Well, don't talk about leaving.  Talk about how a
burning man jumped into the river and came out
frozen like a stick.  The river puts all fire out.  I'm
usually quite good-natured.  Aklavik will stick to
your carcass like a dog to a fish.

ESKER MIKE: *to the crowd*
>Next summer there'll be new boats on the river. American tourists! Men who can't do it anymore and old ladies with veins on their legs and cash in their purses!

SECOND WOMAN:
>Tourists? Where do they tour?

ESKER MIKE:
>Aklavik, you ignoramus! Aklavik! Aklavik! The sinking city! They'll pay you money just to walk into your unpainted shack and see how you live. Take some advice. Don't paint your shack whatever you do.

TOOMIK:
>Some shacks are so full of evil, the paint won't stick on them anyway.

ESKER MIKE:
>The tourists will pay to see Toomik too. They'll pay double!

TOOMIK:
>Pah! You disgust me. I have some good poems three generations old. Fifty cents each. That's a bargain. I have a fresh story about Agiluk and the mate which costs even less.

ESKER MIKE:
>I'll wring the seeds out of your neck!

TOOMIK: *beating her cane in the air*
>Don't strike an old woman!

ESKER MIKE:
>Lies don't hurt.

TOOMIK:

These ears hear things no eyes can see. They saw Agiluk standing in her skin outside the shack. She was screaming at the mosquitoes. Or was it to Nagassuk, who knows how to make a stick act like a man, and long for a stone.

*Oolik weeps.*

ESKER MIKE: *crying out*

Agiluk! That skin is going to be covered with bruises tonight!

*Oolik moans involuntarily and runs by.*

*Esker Mike seizes her by her arm.*

OOLIK: *struggling*

Let me go! Let me go!

*He lets go.*

*She runs off.*

TOOMIK:

That's the story of Agiluk and the mate. You owe me two bits or a White Owl.

ESKER MIKE: *angrily*

You can put it on my credit.

TOOMIK:

Credit? Pah! Look at these arms. Can you read what they say? I'd pay Toomik right now, and then run home before the knife loses its edge on a bird or a tree.

**ESKER MIKE:**
    I'll use the butt of my hand. It's the last boat of the season. I'm going to stay until I can't see it any more.

    *He sits down on a post and sings.*

    Does Idloo kill the dark?
    Idloo is possessed! Idloo is possessed!
    He kills it with a great sleep.

    *To Toomik.*

    Do you have any new verses?

**TOOMIK:**   *singing*
    Does Idloo kill death?
    Idloo is possessed! Idloo is possessed!
    He kills it with a long life.

    Does Idloo kill life?
    Idloo is possessed! Idloo is possessed!
    He kills it with himself.

    Does Idloo kill the cold?
    The cold is possessed! The cold is possessed!
    The cold kills Idloo.

**SECOND WOMAN:**
    It's gone.

**ESKER MIKE:**   *standing up*
    Let's all head for my shack. I need some witnesses.

    *Exit Esker Mike, William, Toomik, the Two Women.*

ADMINISTRATOR:
> I flew to Edmonton.

CONSTABLE:
> I'm from Dauphin.

ADMINISTRATOR:
> Then I flew to Montréal. I had a mistress. A good, dishonest, lovable wench. No morals! She was all that I could handle, but I handled her nicely.

CONSTABLE:
> Okay.

ADMINISTRATOR:
> I ate *blanquette de veau* every Thursday night. And *coq au vin* the rest of the week. I had a suntan as deep as that! I tried to wash it off but I couldn't. I never felt better in my life. And here I am in Aklavik. I don't want to be anywhere else.

CONSTABLE:
> Aklavik! You can stick it up your ass!

ADMINISTRATOR:
> Yes, that's where I have it. In my guts. Take it away and you gut me. Don't you understand? I went to parties in Montréal. The noise was thick enough to touch with your hand. Have you ever felt there were black flies rubbing their legs on the roof of your skull?

CONSTABLE:
> I've never felt like that. I'm thinking about something else.

ADMINISTRATOR:

Be careful then, Constable. Beautiful thoughts are dangerous thoughts when there's so much beauty already. You and I, we're right in the middle of the Great Alluvial Flow. The Mackenzie — Mother of God, and everyone else! Last week I saw J. Christ float by on a raft, wearing a parka and smoking an icicle.

CONSTABLE:

Look, leave me alone.

# At the Shack

*Oolik runs in, distraught.*

OOLIK:

Agiluk!   Agiluk!   *She searches and runs out.*
Agiluk!   *She re-enters.*   He'll kill her! He'll beat
her with the shovel!   *She begins to weep and
tremble, then stops.*   Where's the baby?   Gone!
Where's Natook?   Nobody's here!   *She stoops
down.*   Blood!   It's blood! Everything's clean, but
the blood is wet on the floor. The floor is washed
but the blood is wet. Wet blood!   *She wipes her
hands on her dress.*   Here's some more. It goes out
the door.   *She follows it out.*

# Outside Aklavik

*Agiluk beside two skin-covered mounds.*

*Enter Sergeant Green and Constable MacIntyre.*

*Agiluk is absent-mindedly, fitfully trying to recall a long-forgotten chant.*

CONSTABLE:

There she is. Not as crazy as Esker Mike, but crazy just the same. And two heaps of dead Eskimo. Or is it whale meat? I'll put the cuffs on her now.

SGT. GREEN:

Cuffs? Let's rest awhile, Mac. Things go slow in the North. The ice breaks slow on the River of Disappointment. Fish grow slow. Our justice is slow, though it locks fast, like the grip of frozen brass on a bare hand. This is a funeral. Sit down here on the moss and rest awhile.

*Agiluk tries again to remember the chant, but gives up suddenly and stops.*

SGT. GREEN:
  Hello, Agiluk.

AGILUK:
  Hello, Sergeant Green. Hello, Constable.

SGT. GREEN:
  I smell the smell of summer's end. This is a pleasant time.

AGILUK:
  A time of work. The time to hang up the last of the fish, and bury one's dead.

SGT. GREEN:
  Bury one's dead?

AGILUK:
  As deep as we can, the government says. One foot into the soil that's thawed and the rest to be hacked out with a pick. We threw my father into the river, and you could see him on the bank for years after.

SGT. GREEN:
  Did he look himself, then?

AGILUK:
  He looked himself. In the winter, he was hard and covered with snow and saw nothing but darkness. In the summer his bones appeared and he saw something else. Blind darkness and blinding light! That was my father. It made no difference that he took himself off, one morning, and wouldn't come back.

SGT. GREEN:

    He was a brave man.

AGILUK:

    Brave? He was old. He did what came to him, that day.

       *Silence.*

SGT. GREEN:

    What have you got under those skins?

AGILUK:

    Nothing. Under this one is the body of Natook.

CONSTABLE:

    Natook!

AGILUK:

    He was a strong boy, but he was younger than his brothers. And under this one is the body of Rachel. She was a girl. My mother wanted to kill *me* when I was born.

SGT. GREEN:

    Two less!

AGILUK:

    Two less, and two more. One for the baby that will belong to the mate. And one for the baby I have to give to Esker Mike to balance that one. And if I forget again, I'll take away another of my own, maybe this one that's coming now. I will love my children more, and take them away quick. The same ones. That will stop me. The Northern mate won't want to come close to me then.

    *Sergeant Green looks under the first skin.*

86

SGT. GREEN:
> Was it fast?

AGILUK:
> Fast! The snow knife was sharp. I sharpened it myself. It's hanging from a nail by the stove where it always hangs. You can see for yourself how sharp it is. Blood on one side and blood on the other.

SGT. GREEN:
> Hanging from a nail?

AGILUK:
> By the stove, so the blade won't rust. Ah, Natook! He was only two and he could run like a man. But when his neck is sliced with a knife, a boy doesn't run. He bleeds. It was like opening a muskrat. These hands knew how to do it.

> *Sergeant Green and Constable MacIntyre look under the second skin.*

SGT. GREEN:
> A neat job, indeed. One cut apiece, and small ones at that, considering the task.

CONSTABLE:      *overcome*
> Brutal! Life here is brutal!

SGT. GREEN:
> Not brutal, Mac. Difficult. Life here is difficult. *He contemplates the bodies.*      Twelve years! I feel a hundred years old. Older. Murder falls on me now like an act of peace, like a wet snow falling on an unsuspecting August.

> *Sergeant Green picks up one corpse; Constable MacIntyre the other.*

SGT. GREEN:

Come Rachel! Come Natook! We're off to beautiful Aklavik, where the street moves like a swamp and the sidewalks are made out of wood. And where a Hudson's Bay snow knife covered with blood hangs waiting on a nail.

AGILUK:

Yes, come to my house. And I'll make you a cup of tea.

*Exit.*

# Near the R.C.M.P. Post

*Enter Esker Mike and William.*

WILLIAM:
> It was a good way to kill them. I couldn't have done better myself, and I was born with a knife in my hand.

ESKER MIKE:
> And the police acted like police. Murder anything in Aklavik and Sergeant Green will be there. Though it doesn't compare to the time they got Albert Johnson up Eagle River. That was something! Two constables shot through the gut! And a soldier!

WILLIAM:
> Two constables! Two men of the law!

ESKER MIKE:
> They didn't take *him* to Edmonton. No hospital and good food for Albert Johnson. Only snow in his mouth.

WILLIAM: *dolefully*

They might as well shoot Agiluk too. When the hot summer comes, she'll grow sick, and that will be the end.

ESKER MIKE:

You're right. It's no use waiting for her. Maybe we'll move in with Oolik. She's Agiluk's step-sister, and she has a stove that could burn the ears off an ice-worm.

PRODUCTION NOTES:

The action takes place in and near Aklavik, Northwest Territories, in the early 1960's.

The "u" in Agiluk, Tulugak, Inuk, etc. is pronounced as in "flute" except for muktuk, where it is pronounced as in "duck." "Lynx" in the singular is pronounced, in trapper's parlance, "link." The standard and familiar pronunciation is "links."

An intermission may be held following the scene with the Minister of Northern Affairs.